IT'S A WEIRD,
WEIRD SCHOOL

IT'S A
WEIRD, WEIRD
SCHOOL

Stephen Mooser

A Yearling Book

Published by
Dell Publishing
a division of
Bantam Doubleday Dell Publishing Group, Inc.
666 Fifth Avenue
New York, New York 10103

The trademark Yearling® is registered in the U.S. Patent and Trademark Office.

The trademark Dell® is registered in the U.S. Patent and Trademark Office.

ISBN: 0-440-40500-9

Reprinted by arrangement with Delacorte Press

Printed in the United States of America

September 1991

10 9 8 7 6 5 4 3 2 1

OPM

*For the students at CAVE,
and for the teachers who made it possible,
Anita Dobbs, Dan Foster, and
Dr. Etta Mooser*

CONTENTS

IT'S A WEIRD,
WEIRD SCHOOL

1

THE DEAD
MAN IN THE CAR

My friend, my good friend Jamie Plufphanger, collected, passed on, and—worse yet—actually believed, some of the most preposterous stories ever told. One day, for instance, she said, "Carrie, do you remember my cousin Katy?"

"Not really," I said.

"Katy," she said. "The one with the frizzy brown hair, the long skinny nose, and the big ears, You know, the one who looks just like you."

I rubbed my finger up along my nose and sighed. "Yeah, what about her?"

"Well," said Jamie, lowering her voice, "Katy had a friend who sprayed her hair every day. Every single day."

"So?" I said.

"So," Jamie went on, "she never washed her hair because it was never messed up. The fool. Pretty soon bugs began living underneath all that spray. And after about six months they ate through to her brain and killed her! Can you believe it?"

Frankly, I couldn't. But then, according to Jamie, the world was full of such happenings. To her the strange, the weird, and the bizarre were the stuff of everyday life.

One of her most fantastic stories is the one I want to tell you now. It's a story that began the month I got kicked out of school, had my picture on the front page of the paper, and finally ended up on national TV.

It was all too bizarre to be true, and like any great story, it couldn't wait. I suppose that's why Jamie had to pick the morning of Mrs. Pride's literature exam to lean over and whisper to me the startling details.

"Carrie," she began, "there's a three-year-old Corvette down at Sam Davidson's Used Cars that's for sale for two hundred dollars. After school we got to hustle down there and get it."

I shot Jamie a murderous stare and hunched back over my notes. I was trying to memorize the plot of a story called "The Haunted Castle" and Jamie was trying to sell me a used car. At thirteen I wasn't even old enough to drive. And at four foot eleven I was probably too short as well. Besides, I needed the study time. I had no intention of getting an F on the test.

Of course, for Jamie an F on the test would be no big deal. She was probably going to get one anyway. But I needed an A if I was to be Madison County School Board president. Next week the town was holding its annual Youth Runs the City Day. Maybe you have the same sort of thing in your town. It's a day when kids get to run the city. Harold Preston was going to be the mayor. A girl from the high school had been picked as police chief, and since I had the top grades at Madison Junior High, I was going to be head of the School Board. It was all for fun, but it was a real honor, and I didn't want anything to screw up my grades before I got the job.

"Listen," Jamie whispered again, "if we're there first we can clean it up and sell it tomorrow for five thousand dollars, at least."

"Shhhh," I hissed. "I'm trying to study."

"It's so cheap because of the smell."

Mrs. Pride cleared her throat and began passing out the test.

Jamie stared at her desk—but only till Mrs. Pride's back was turned. Then she went on whispering, "The guy that used to own it was driving out through

the Mojave Desert last month and had a heart at-
tack. The air-conditioning was on and all the win-
dows were rolled up. The car went off the road and
sat there for nearly three weeks.''

''So?'' I said.

''So? So!'' whispered Jamie, now leaning in so
close, I could see the tiny red and blue foil flakes
she'd sprinkled into her curly brown hair. ''So they
can't get the smell of death out of that car. It's in
everything, the steering wheel, the seats, even the
engine. That's why the car is only two hundred
bucks.''

''Can we discuss this after the test?'' I asked as
we both received the test from Mrs. Pride, a single
sheet of paper.

''We could clean it up, I know,'' Jamie whispered.
She was nearly out of her seat. ''A friend of my
mom's got this new cleaner that will take the smell
out of anything. No one else knows about it. She
makes it up special. Don't you see? We got the
inside track!''

''Shhhhhhh,'' hissed perfect Miss Amy Burke from
across the aisle. Amy was going to be on the School
Board with me because her grades were nearly iden-
tical to mine. If I fell down, Amy was next in line
for the presidency. ''Be quiet,'' she said, shaking
her pencil in our direction. ''Some of us are trying
to take a test.''

Jamie sank back into her seat. "We can talk after the test," I whispered.

"Forget the test," she shot back. "We'll make enough money so that you'll never have to go to school again. Thousands, girl. Thousands!"

I hated to admit it, but Jamie was starting to get my interest. "This isn't another one of your stories, is it?"

Jamie pressed her hand to her heart. "I swear it's true. There was an ad for the car in the paper this morning. A friend of my brother's saw it."

"How do you know someone hasn't already bought it?"

Jamie rolled her big green eyes. "Carrie, don't be so dumb. Why do you think that car is only two hundred dollars? Nobody can get that smell out of it."

"And you think this cleaner of yours will do the job?"

"Didn't I tell you it's a secret formula?" Jamie raised her eyebrows. "It's not common knowledge, but the woman who invented it is supposed to be a witch."

"A witch, really?"

I felt a hand tighten on the back of my neck.

"Carrie Burns, how could you?"

I tried to turn around, but Mrs. Pride had me pinned in place. I'd been so interested in the death car, I hadn't seen her sneaking up.

"How could you cheat in my class!"

"But, Mrs. Pride . . ."

"I heard you two talking. Don't think I didn't hear you tell Jamie just now that 'The Haunted Castle' opens up with witches."

"Mrs. Pride?" said Jamie.

"Keep your mouth shut, Jamie Lee Plufphanger. I don't doubt you're the cause of this."

"Mrs. Pride, please, let me explain . . ." I said.

"Don't make matters worse than they already are," she replied, releasing her hand from my neck and simultaneously sweeping up my paper. Then, adding Jamie's paper to my own, she crumpled them both up and walked to the front of the room, where she deposited them both in the wastepaper basket. "F's," she said. "And count yourselves lucky I'm not having you expelled."

THE DEATH
CAR

When the bell rang the students swept out the door as if carried on the winds of a tornado. Before the last shouts had died away and as Paul Prentice's paper was still settling toward Mrs. Pride's desk, I swallowed hard and walked to the front of the room.

Clearing my throat, I said, "I'm sorry, but I wasn't cheating. We were just talking, Jamie and me."

Mrs. Pride busily shuffled the papers into a pile and didn't look up.

"You know I don't need to cheat," I continued.

At last, the papers in order, she looked up and studied me silently, shaking her head slowly. She was about forty-five, but she had enough gray hairs for a woman of sixty, a result, I'm sure, of her many years at the junior high.

"How could you have cheated?" she finally said sadly. "Carrie, I'm terribly disappointed."

"Mrs. Pride," I said, screwing up my courage, "I can't afford an F. I want to be School Board head next week, and I got to have an A for that."

"Then maybe you shouldn't have tried to help out Jamie Plufphanger," she said. "It's certainly no secret that cheaters are not tolerated in this class."

"But we weren't even talking about 'The Haunted Castle,' " I said.

"I'm sorry, Carrie. I really am," she said. "But you know the rules. Now, please, run along. I've got papers to grade."

"But, Mrs. Pride—"

"Run along, Carrie."

I sighed, picked up my books, and walked out into the hall. I was more depressed than I'd been in a long, long time. Here it was the end of April, with school winding down, and my perfect grades were ruined. You might have thought that Jamie would have been a little apologetic. But she was so excited about that death car that I don't think she paid the incident the slightest mind. In fact, she didn't pay the slightest mind to a lot of things, including the way she dressed. Today, for instance, she was wearing a red bow tie, a skirt made up of some kind of patchwork burlap, and different-colored socks. I called it a mess, but Jamie called it style.

Despite our differences Jamie and I had been best friends for nearly the entire year. In fact, I'd liked her from the moment I first saw her stroll into Mr. Templeton's math class wearing a tennis shoe on one foot and a sandal on the other.

She was waiting when I came out into the hall.

"What'd she say?" she asked.

"Nothing," I said, feeling spaced, and somewhat dazed. "I swear, if this screws up my School Board job ..." I bared my teeth. "Jamie Plufphanger, this is all your fault!"

Jamie smiled back through her braces. "Carrie, I swear, you're a bigger worrywart than my brother, Luke. In less than an hour you'll be thanking me. Come on, we got to get that car before someone else beats us to it."

I sighed and let Jamie lead me out of the school and across the street to where we got on the number ten bus bound for town.

We rode most of the way in silence, Jamie alone with her thoughts of impending riches, and me with my fears of impending doom.

Finding Sam Davidson's car lot was about as easy as locating the sky. Mr. Davidson was the biggest car dealer in town, and every intersection of Ventura and Fulton streets was full of his cars. Red and white plastic flags fluttered above the lots, and above the flags spun a huge sign advertising Mr. Davidson's QUALITY USED AUTOMOBILES, as well as his money-back guarantee.

The bus dropped us off on the southwest corner, but we crossed the street to the main lot and started looking around for the bargain Stinkmobile.

"There're no Corvettes on the lot," I said. "Jamie, if you got me—"

"Have faith, have faith," said Jamie. She stuck her tiny turned-up nose in the air and sniffed. "It's here, all right, but they got it hidden."

I sniffed the air but only came up with the faint scents of car wax and grease.

"You don't think they'd just leave it outside, do you?" she said. "No, they got it tucked away somewhere so that it won't scare off the regular customers."

I sniffed the air again but couldn't pick up even the slightest scent of death. "Jamie, I feel like a fool."

Jamie gave me her all-knowing smile, then winked to emphasize her confidence. "Trust me," she said.

A heavyset bald man in a blue-and-white seersucker suit suddenly emerged from behind a row of trucks and greeted us with a toothy smile. "Hello, young ladies. Looking for something?"

Jamie glanced around to make sure we were alone. Then, lowering her voice, she said, ''We're interested in the Corvette. The one in the paper.''

The salesman leaned in close. Apparently Jamie had either dropped her voice too much, or the salesman was slightly deaf.

''The Corvette,'' Jamie repeated. ''The one for two hundred dollars.''

The salesman smiled and shook his head.

''You know, the death car,'' said Jamie. ''We're prepared to pay cash.''

''Death car?'' the salesman repeated.

I was beginning to feel like an almighty fool when the salesman surprised me by adding, ''You mean the one the fellow died in out in the desert?''

''Yeah, yeah,'' said Jamie.

''The one the guy sat in for a month till the smell was even drilled into the engine block?'' he continued.

''That's it,'' said Jamie. ''Was he in there a whole month?''

The salesman pulled a toothpick out of the breast pocket of his jacket and began picking at his teeth.

''Could we see it?'' I asked.

''Don't think so,'' he said.

''We won't mind the smell,'' said Jamie. ''And, like I said, we can get the cash.''

''Our friend said the price was two hundred dollars,'' I added.

The salesman worked at his teeth and let us go on

for a minute or two till he finally said, "Listen, girls, I don't know who started this crazy story, but there ain't a lick of truth in it. Umpteen kids have been on this lot today asking after that car, and I suspect about a hundred others have called on the phone."

Jamie and I exchanged confused glances. "But what about the ad in the paper?"

"What ad is that?" he said. "Did you actually see it yourself?"

Jamie narrowed her eyes and drew back her head as if she could see through him to the truth. "My friend saw it."

"Listen," he said, "I got better things to do than sell phantom cars to teenagers. You bring me that ad, and then we'll talk. Okay?"

I felt my face begin to flush. Jamie had made me feel like a fool for the second time in one day. "Let's go," I said.

But Jamie didn't seem the least bit put off. "We'll be back with the ad," she said confidently.

"You do that," said the salesman. "And one more thing. You tell everyone at your school to stop pestering us. There ain't no such thing as a two-hundred-dollar Corvette, and there never was."

On the way back to the bus stop I felt like clunking Jamie Plufphanger on the head with my book bag. "You ruined my day and wasted my afternoon," I muttered. "From now on I'm not listening to anything you say—ever."

Jamie gave me that sugary smile of hers and clapped me on the back. "Carrie, Carrie. I'm surprised. Would I lead you wrong? Think about it. That salesman was lying through his teeth. Sure as anything that car's stuck back in one of Davidson's garages. Didn't I tell you I smelled something funny?"

"Then why didn't he sell it to us if he's got it?" I asked.

"Gosh, Carrie. Sometimes you're so dumb. He didn't sell it 'cause he probably got hold of the same cleaning formula we were going to use. I once heard if you advertise something you got to sell it at that price. My guess is that he plans to clean up the car, ship it to another city, and unload it at the full price." She slapped me on the back again and added, "Hey, makes sense, doesn't it?"

"No," I said. "Frankly, it doesn't." Then, giving Jamie an exaggerated smile of my own, I added, "From now on, please, I beg you, no more great deals."

By the time the bus dropped me off on Maroa Street, a block from my house, it was nearly six o'clock. And by the time I walked into the house, dinner was on the table and Mom and Dad had already sat down to eat.

"Carrie, where have you been?" asked Mom, looking up from a plate, half of which was drenched in purple.

Not again, I thought to myself. Beets.

Dad looked up from the papers stacked alongside his plate and smiled. "Sit down, sweetie, sit down," he said. "How was school?"

I pulled out my chair and sat down. I knew Dad didn't require an answer. His face was buried again in the legal papers he'd brought home from work.

"Was there a club meeting or something?" asked Mom. She plopped a big spoonful of beets onto my plate. Then added a hamburger patty and a little salad.

"I went down to a car lot with Jamie," I said. "We were going to buy a car. It was nearly brand new, and only two hundred dollars."

"Sounds like quite a bargain," said Mom, smiling. "But, dear, you don't drive."

"We were just going to clean it up, then resell it," I said. "Jamie thought we'd make a fortune."

Dad's nose rose from the paper like a submarine coming to the surface. "A fortune, you say?"

"It turned out to be nothing. A stupid rumor, that's all. Anyway, it's too gruesome to talk about at dinner."

Mom gave me a sideways glance and attacked her beets.

"That Jamie's full of schemes and ideas, isn't she?" said Dad. "I like that in a girl."

"It's because she's desperate," I said. "More than anything she wants to get out of school. She figures if she can somehow hit it big, she can retire before graduation."

"What does she have against school?" asked Mom.

"Everything," I said. "Jamie likes doing stuff on her own, and ever since Mr. Corliss took over as principal, that place has been run like a prison."

Mom frowned. "Surely it can't be that bad, dear."

I chewed on a piece of hamburger for a while, then I said, "It's pretty bad. They never let you do anything that's not part of Mr. Corliss's dumb schedule. He's cut out almost all the electives so all we get is English, math, a little bit of language, and some social studies. No art, no science, and barely any PE. Jamie's smart enough. She could get good grades, but she's just not interested in the things they're teaching."

"So does she get bad grades?" asked Mom.

"She got an F today in Mrs. Pride's class," I said.

As Mom was shaking her head, I added, "I did too."

"Oh?" said Dad. I'd caught his attention once again.

"Jamie and I were talking during a test and Mrs. Pride thought we were cheating," I explained. "She got real mad, grabbed our papers, and gave us both

F's.'' I rearranged the beets on my plate. ''I'm afraid it may cost me the School Board presidency.''

''Oh, that would be a shame,'' said Mom.

''In my humble opinion it would most likely also be illegal,'' said Dad. ''They made you a verbal promise, and I think we could make that stand up in court.''

''Dad, I don't want to sue over it.''

''You have to stick up for your rights,'' said Dad. I don't think a day ever went by that he didn't threaten to sue someone. ''You can't let them push you around. A court order, perhaps an injunction, and we'll have them begging for you to serve on their board.'' Dad returned to his papers. ''They give you any trouble, just come talk to me,'' he muttered.

''Sure, Dad,'' I said. *But to get his undivided attention I'll probably need an appointment,* I thought.

3

PIRATE GOLD

The next day in class Mrs. Pride didn't mention anything to me about my paper. The fact of the matter was that she didn't mention anything at all. I'd never known her to be so cold. She acted as if I weren't even in the room. It was as if she'd disowned me or something.

I was determined to talk to her after class, but Jamie was just as determined to talk to me.

Grabbing me by the arm, she pulled me to the side just as I was heading for Mrs. Pride's desk. As the rest of the class swept by us toward the door, Jamie whispered, "Our fortune's made. I was in the library this morning, doing some reading for history, and I came across something that's worth a million bucks—at least."

I looked at Mrs. Pride piling up her books. In a moment she'd be out the door. "Jamie," I said, "I want to talk to Mrs. Pride. I don't want to hear about any two-hundred-dollar death cars, okay?"

Jamie pulled me in close till we were nose to nose, eye to eye. "This isn't some half-baked rumor I'm telling you. Not some wild, far-out scheme. Not this time, Carrie."

"I bet," I said, watching Mrs. Pride sail out the door.

"I swear. I know just where we can find a million dollars in gold," Jamie persisted.

"Sure. Where?"

Jamie looked about the deserted room and tightened her grip on my arm. "Right here in the building. In the library!"

Then, before I could say "yougottabecrazy," Jamie had me down the hall and through the front door of the school library. No one was at the librarian's desk as we passed by, but I heard voices from behind the stacks and recognized one of them as belonging to the librarian, old Mr. Proctor.

"You're not going to believe what I found this morning during my remedial reading class," said

Jamie, dragging me back into the stacks. "This has just got to be the luckiest day of my entire life, I swear."

Reaching behind a row of Lincoln biographies, Jamie fished out a worn leather-bound book with faded red lettering on the spine.

"You found a million dollars in a book about Abraham Lincoln?" I said.

She waved the book in my face. "No, stupid. I only hid it over here so that no one else would find it. This isn't about Lincoln. It's about a place called Cocos Island, off the coast of Central America. A place, you might be interested to know, in which there is buried a fabulous pirate treasure."

Glancing about to make sure we weren't being observed, she opened the book and began slowly fanning through the pages. "You're not going to believe what I found," she said. "It's just going to blow you away."

I tapped my foot impatiently as I waited for the unveiling of Jamie's latest get-rich-quick scheme.

"Here!" she said triumphantly, opening the book to a full-page map of Cocos Island. "Take a look at this."

I took the book from Jamie and looked down at the simple black-and-white map of a small pear-shaped island. There certainly wasn't anything unusual about the map itself, but there was something extraordinary written across the top in shaky handwriting. These are the words, as precisely as I can remember them: *I, Peg-Leg Bones, swear on a barrel of rum that I helped bury Captain Kidd's treasure on Cocos Island. No one is left but me to tell the tale. So, matey, if ye find this map, then the treasure be yours. Remember, X marks the spot.* And it was signed with a flourish by Peg-Leg Bones himself.

"And there it is," said Jamie, pointing to a tiny *X* at the top of the island. "That's where we'll dig."

"Wow, Jamie," I said. "Maybe you are onto something this time. If—"

"You get out of my library!" came a sudden scream. I nearly dropped the book, and jerked my head around to see if we were the ones being yelled at.

Peeking through the bookcase, I saw old Mr. Proctor, the librarian. He was shaking and pointing at a thin man with a thick mustache and a red, pocked face. I recognized him at once as Homer Brant, head of the School Board. The man whose job I was supposed to take over in exactly one week.

"Begone!" shouted Mr. Proctor. His thin white hair, always a mess, stood out now, almost as if it were electrified. His blue eyes were cold and piercing. "And don't ever, ever try to tell me again what books I can and cannot have in my library."

Brant's face reddened another degree and he raised himself up on the toes of his polished brown wing tips. "We'll see what my committee says about the trash you're carrying in this library, Proctor. And, believe me, we'll see about you as well!''

"I'll be looking forward to the report," snapped Mr. Proctor.

"Huumph!" snorted Mr. Brant, clicking his heels. And without another word he spun around and stomped out of the room.

Openmouthed, I turned to Jamie and found her staring back, wide-eyed. We were both in shock.

"What do you suppose that was all about?" I whispered.

"I don't know," she whispered back. "But I think we'd better get out of here."

"What about the map?" I said.

Jamie smiled and tapped her forehead. "Photographic memory," she said. "It's all up here."

"Then, put back the book," I said. "I don't want to run into Proctor when he's on the rampage."

"Aye, aye, mate," she said. She gave me a wink and a short, snappy salute as she shoved the book onto the shelf too hard. The book banged into the books on the other side and sent a slew of them clattering to the floor. The noise was enough to raise the ghost of Captain Kidd himself.

"Who's back there!" came Proctor's low, gravelly voice. "Come on out!"

Jamie and I exchanged looks of sheer panic. Looks that were still on our faces when Mr. Proctor discovered us just moments later.

"Pick up the mess," he said. "Sorry I yelled. For a moment I thought you were Mr. Brant, come back to burn my books."

Mr. Proctor looked as if he needed someone to talk to, and Jamie and I were only too glad to listen.

"Brant is head of a committee called the Citizens for Decency," he explained. "They come around here all the time, skimming through the books and clucking their tongues. They've got a list a mile long of books they'd like to see banned. So far I've held them off, but I don't think that can last. If I don't start tossing out books, I think Brant means to have me canned."

Jamie raised her eyebrows and gave her lips a lick. "What kind of books does he want to ban? Anything ... you know ... juicy?"

"Hardly, though Brant might disagree," explained Mr. Proctor. "*Huckleberry Finn,* for one, most of Judy Blume's books, and, naturally, *Catcher in the Rye.*"

"*Catcher in the Rye?*" said Jamie. "Wait a minute, what do they have against Holden Caulfield? He's a great character."

"He is a great character. A lot like you, Jamie. But he's too independent for Brant. Caulfield is a thinker, and people with minds of their own don't sit well with the Citizens for Decency."

"I sure hope you don't lose your job over this,' said Jamie.

Mr. Proctor sat down on the edge of his desk and brushed back his white hair. "Brant is a powerful man in this town. And I'm ... well, I'm just a librarian."

"This whole thing's just awful," I said. "You know, my father's an attorney and maybe—"

"Sam? Excuse me," came a voice from the hallway. We all looked up and saw a squinty-eyed bald head thrust into the open doorway. It was almost like something out of a science fiction movie except we all knew the head was attached to the plump body of our principal, Mr. Corliss. "Could I see you in my office?"

Mr. Proctor snorted to himself and gave the principal a look of undisguised contempt. "When do you want to see me?"

The principal clucked his tongue and shook his head. "Now, Sam, right away."

Proctor shoved himself off the desk and ambled slowly toward the door.

Mr. Corliss looked at his watch and said, "Step lively, Sam, I've only got six and a half minutes till my next appointment." And with that he disappeared back into the hallway.

"You got my sympathy, Mr. Proctor," said Jamie. "I've gone to the principal's office a few times myself. And it's noooooo fun."

Proctor paused at the door and smoothed down his hair with his hand. "Corliss doesn't have the backbone of a squid.'' he said. ''I think Brant has talked him into firing me.''

''Fire you? For protecting your books?'' I said. ''Isn't that a librarian's job?''

Mr. Proctor smiled, shook his head, and vanished into the hallway.

Silently I wished him well, but it was a wasted wish. The next morning the library was locked and Mr. Proctor was nowhere to be found.

4

THE GREAT
LIBRARY RAID

By morning everyone at Madison had heard about
Mr. Proctor's suspension and the library's closing.
Some of the kids seemed upset, but there were many
others who didn't seem the least concerned.

One who did care was Jamie. I ran into her on my
way to Mrs. Pride's class. She was knocking on the
glass in the library door and crying to be let in.

"Jamie," I said, "didn't you hear? They suspended Proctor. There's no one there."

Jamie gave me a quick smile and said, "No, someone's inside, all right, but they won't answer the door. See for yourself.''

What I saw when I peeked through the glass nearly shocked me out of my pink knee-highs. Jamie was right, someone was in the library. Mr. Corliss was holding a box of books. As I watched, two women I'd never seen before, both heavily made up and wearing velour jogging suits, appeared from behind the stacks, carrying books, which they put in the box held by Mr. Corliss.

I was almost certain it was the Citizens for Decency Committee, and a second later I was sure of it when Mr. Brant, his face red and sweaty, appeared with an armload of more supposedly dangerous books.

I was stunned, shocked, and more than a little outraged. ''Jamie, we've got to stop them.''

''I'm trying,'' said Jamie, ''but they won't open the door.''

As if on cue Mr. Corliss turned to the door and waved at us angrily. Pointing to his watch, he shouted, ''Class is about to start. Go! Go!''

''This is terrible,'' I said, ignoring the principal.

''It's worse than terrible,'' said Jamie. ''I'm almost certain that lady in the blue sweat pants grabbed the Cocos Island book. If she burns it, I'm dead. That map was my ticket out of here.''

I gave my head a tap. ''I thought you had it all up here.''

Jamie rolled her eyes. ''So no one's perfect, okay? I'm telling you, this is one huge disaster.''

Now I was really fuming. "Jamie, this is a disaster, all right, but not because of your stupid map. Is money all you think about?"

Jamie pounded on the glass. "Hey, that map is worth a million bucks, at least," she said. She pounded some more, harder. "You'd be upset too. Wouldn't you, huh?"

"Yeah, but Mr. Proctor's gone and now they're taking away our books," I argued. "They're taking away our freedom to read!"

Just then a third person joined us at the window. It was Amy Burke, whom I could have recognized with my eyes closed from the stench of her ghastly perfume.

"Yoo-hoo," she chirped, elbowing us aside so that she could rap on the window. "Mother, hi!"

A woman with bright red lipstick turned about and waved cheerily to Amy. "Run along to class, dear. See you later."

"That's my mom," said Amy. "She's helping clean up the library."

"The way I see it, she's stealing our books," said Jamie.

"And the way I see it, she helped get Mr. Proctor suspended," I added.

"Serves him right," Amy said. "That library was full of filthy books."

As always, there was no filth on Amy. From the polished glasses she wore on top of her head to the blinding white tennis shoes on her tiny feet, she was as spotless as a tub full of bleach.

"Amy," I said, "did you ever read any of those books that the Citizens for Decency wanted to ban?"

"Heavens, no!" she exclaimed, a perfectly manicured hand going to her perfectly formed mouth. "I wouldn't want to even touch one for fear I'd get some horrible disease."

"If you haven't read them, then how can you know they're dirty?" I asked.

"Because Mr. Brant says so," says Amy. "He knows what's best for me, I'm sure. Otherwise he wouldn't be head of the School Board."

"Amy," I said, "sometimes, I swear ..."

"Carrie," she replied sarcastically, "—swear, swear swear. Is that all you know how to do?"

Before I could reply, the bell rang. Jamie gave the window one last pounding and screamed, "There's a book in there on Cocos Island. Keep your mitts off of it. It's mine, you thieving lunkheads. It's mine!"

"Jamie," said Amy angrily, "my mother is not a thief. Now, you take that back!"

"You're right," said Jamie. She bowed low. "I was out of line. She's not a thief. Just a lunkhead."

The bell rang again and we hurried off for class with Amy and Jamie trading insults and threats all the way down the hallway and through the door.

5

THE BACKBONE OF
A SQUID

Mrs. Pride was the only teacher that day who I
heard mention Mr. Proctor and the closing of the
library. In fact, she went beyond just discussing it;
she suggested we take some kind of action.

"As a literature teacher I'm particularly offended
by the actions of the Citizens for Decency," she told
our seventh-period class. "And all of you should be
too. The Bill of Rights promises us freedom of the
press. And history shows that those who don't stand

up for their rights inevitably end up losing them. We can't let this outrageous act go unanswered.''

''What can we do?'' asked Eric Ressler, the biggest boy in the class, though maybe not the smartest. I was surprised he was so interested in the library. I don't think he'd read a book all year.

''I'm sure there are many things we can do,'' said Mrs. Pride. ''Anyone have a suggestion?''

Amy Burke's opinion was that maybe we shouldn't do anything at all. ''Don't you think that Mr. Brant knows what's best for the school?''

''Perhaps he does,'' said Mrs. Pride, ''but I wish he'd discussed it with us first.'' Then she added, ''Amy, I know your mother is part of the Citizens' Committee, and I'm sure she means well, but it's not fair for her to tell the rest of us what is proper to read.''

Paul Prentice, a tall, long-haired boy with thick glasses who sat in the front row, suggested that we take an ax and reopen the library by breaking down the door.

''Yeah,'' said Jamie. ''Now you're talking.''

A couple of other kids also thought it was a fine idea, one of them even offering to run home for the ax.

Mrs. Pride sat on the edge of her desk and watched the discussion unfold. There was a gleam in her eye the likes of which I hadn't seen in some time. I think having a cause to fight for had inspired her, had inspired us. Madison Junior High was, for the most part, an incredibly dull place. Ever since Mr. Corliss had taken over and abolished everything but the basics, the fun parts of school had become but distant memories. Maybe it was all very efficient, but it was also very boring. Now, suddenly, with Mr. Proctor's dismissal, something new and different was happening and all of us, even the teacher, could feel the adrenaline starting to flow.

"What about a petition?" I offered. "We can demand that Mr. Proctor come back and the library be reopened, sign it at the bottom, and take it down to Mr. Corliss."

"I still like the idea of the ax," said Paul. There was an excited tone to his voice which, combined with his talk of the ax, made everyone a little uneasy.

"An ax is the only way to attract these people's attention," said Eric. "They won't understand anything else."

In the end Mrs. Pride went along with my suggestion, finally winning the day with a quote from a play called *Richelieu*. "The pen," she said, "is mightier than the sword—or, in this case, the ax."

We spent the remainder of the class composing the petition, in which we demanded that Mr. Proctor be reinstated, the library be reopened, and all the books be returned. Except for Amy Burke and a few others, most everyone signed it.

At the end of the day I accompanied Mrs. Pride to Mr. Corliss's office, where we planned to deliver the petition in person.

Mrs. Omani, the principal's secretary, an incredibly thin woman with a long face and a nose as sharp as a hatchet, was busily constructing a paper-clip chain when we walked into the office.

"Priscilla," said Mrs. Pride, "we'd like to see Mr. Corliss for a few moments. Would you tell him we're here?"

Mrs. Omani gritted her teeth as she forced another paper clip onto the chain. Without looking up she asked, "What da ya need?"

Mrs. Pride slowly repeated, "We need to see Mr. Corliss. Now."

Priscilla Omani pursed her lips and narrowed her eyes. "Well, I gotta tell him what it's about."

"It's about the library," said Mrs. Pride. "It'll only take a moment."

I was nervous as it was, and Mrs. Omani wasn't making things any easier. My hands were so damp, I was afraid I was going to make the ink on the petition run.

"Please," I said, "could we see Mr. Corliss? It's very important."

"You telling me what to do?" snapped Mrs. Omani.

She turned to Mrs. Pride. ''You know I don't have to take orders from students.''

''Priscilla''—Mrs. Pride sighed—''just tell him we're here.''

''Oh, all right,'' she said, dropping the chain to her desk and getting to her feet. ''But you don't have an appointment, so don't be surprised if he won't see you.''

Mrs. Omani knocked on the big oak door marked PRINCIPAL and Mrs. Pride looked at me, smiling and shaking her head. I smiled and shook my head in return. It was good to be friends with her again, and I had Mr. Corliss and his stubborn secretary to thank for our reconciliation. I must say the one positive thing about having a principal as bad as Mr. Corliss is that it brings everyone else together. It gives almost everyone something in common.

Mrs. Omani disappeared into the office and when she came out a few minutes later she was accompanied by Mr. Corliss, his bald head gleaming like a gum ball and his potbelly hiding his belt. Glancing at his watch, he plastered a smile on his face and said, ''Mrs. Omani says you want to discuss the library. Go. You've got precisely three and one half minutes.''

''Three and a half minutes?'' said Mrs. Pride. ''Mr. Corliss, we've come to you about a very serious situation.''

"At three twenty-two every day I have to call in the attendance figures to the state," he explained. "As you know, the school receives its funding based on the number of pupils attending school each day. I can assure you there is nothing more serious than getting that money. This school needs every penny it can get." He glanced at his watch again. "Three minutes."

Mrs. Pride took a deep breath and drew herself up to her full height. "Mr. Corliss," she began, "many of us at Madison are very concerned about what's been going on at the library. Carrie Burns, representing most of the students in my seventh-period literature class, has something she'd like to give you." Mrs. Pride nodded to me. "Carrie?"

Trying my best to look Mr. Corliss in the eye, I handed him the petition. "We're asking you to reopen the library and also to reinstate Mr. Proctor," I said. "As you can see, there are quite a few signatures on our petition."

"And we're also asking that you return the books that were taken out of there today by the Citizens for Decency," added Mrs. Pride.

Mr. Corliss glanced at the petition, then at his watch. "Uh-uh. This is a fine petition, Carrie, but, uh, I don't think I can do what you want."

"And why not?" said Mrs. Pride. "Is it because you let Mr. Brant and Mrs. Burke bully you? I'm sorry, Mr. Corliss, but closing the library was wrong, and possibly even illegal.''

''Now, now,'' said the principal, raising his hand and stepping backward toward his office. ''Don't be making threats unless you've got all the details.''

''Like what?'' I said, feeling suddenly bold. ''Tell us.''

''I can't, I'm afraid,'' he said. ''It's confidential, in fact.''

''Yeah,'' I said, ''I bet.''

''Carrie Burns!'' snapped Mrs. Omani, suddenly coming to life. ''Watch the way you speak to your principal.''

Mr. Corliss glanced desperately into his office. He looked to me as if he might have been contemplating an escape. Mr. Proctor had been right. The fatso didn't have the backbone of a squid.

''The truth of the matter is that it's out of my hands. When the School Board meets on Monday they'll take up the matter and decide on whether Sam Proctor is qualified to continue as librarian.''

''I wish you hadn't felt it necessary to take this to the board,'' said Mrs. Pride. ''Mr. Brant isn't exactly sympathetic to Sam Proctor.''

''Wait a minute,'' I said. ''Monday is Youth Day. The board isn't even meeting, only the students.''

Mr. Corliss smiled. If he had been closer, he would have patted me on the head as well. It was that kind

37

of what-a-naive-little-girl-you-are smile. "The students only sit on the board for a few minutes," he said. "The rest of the time the regular members are conducting business."

"Oh," I said.

Mr. Corliss wrinkled his huge brow. "Carrie, is it true you're not going to be board president? Mrs. Burke told me that Amy said you failed a test or something. Is that right?"

I lowered my head and shrugged my shoulders. There was a moment's silence. Then I heard Mrs. Pride say, "No, no, it's not true. That was merely a misunderstanding."

I looked at Mrs. Pride and my mouth flopped open. I was speechless.

"Carrie had perfect grades this year," Mrs. Pride continued. "On Monday she'll be School Board president. You can be sure of it."

"Well, I'm glad to hear that," Mr. Corliss said. I knew he was lying. Then, taking another two steps backward, he glanced one more time at his watch, drew in his breath, and said, "Well ... thanks for your concern about the library." Easing himself into his office, he waved the petition at us. "I'm looking forward to reading this. Really. Thanks for coming by."

He smiled one last time and then slammed the door in our faces. For a moment I stood rooted in place. I couldn't decide whether I was going to be ecstatic because Mrs. Pride had taken back my F, or to be bitter about the way Mr. Corliss had ignored our demands.

In the end I was bitter. "Eric was right," I said. "The only way to get their attention is with an ax."

Mrs. Omani gasped, and we turned and walked out the door.

6

ANOTHER
COLORFUL MEAL

The theme color for dinner that night was yellow: scrambled eggs, yellow Rice-a-Roni, and corn muffins. Dessert, I was almost certain, was going to be lemon pudding.

"Mrs. Pride changed my grade from an F to an A," I announced to my parents. "I think we're friends again."

"Does that mean you'll be School Board head on Monday?" asked my mother.

"Uh-huh," I replied, "but it's not as big a deal as

41

I thought. We only get to be in charge for a few minutes.''

Dad put down the pen he'd been using to mark the papers next to his plate and flicked a bit of egg out of his mustache. ''If you use your time wisely, a few minutes can go a long way,'' he said. ''Think of how many people would love to be President, if only for thirty seconds. You could do a lot in that time.''

''Yeah, like blow up the world,'' I said.

''You'll have power,'' said Dad. ''Big power. Once you get hold of that School Board, you're in charge, remember that. That's the law.''

''The law?'' I said.

''Maybe not precisely, but lawyers have a way of making the truth out of most anything. As I've said before, if you get into trouble, you can just call on me.''

I smiled. ''Thanks, Dad,'' I said. But he may not have heard me, because by the time the words were out of my mouth, his head was once again buried in his legal papers.

Mom reached across the table and patted me on the hand. ''Dear, you wouldn't really blow up the world, would you?''

I put a devilish grin on my face and pretended I was giving the matter some thought. I waited till Mom looked real worried, then said, ''Nah, but I do wish I could do something for Mr. Proctor.''

''From what you told us before dinner, it looks

pretty hopeless,'' said Mom. ''You said Mr. Corliss didn't even consider your petition.''

''All he cares about is his schedule and his state attendance money. I tell you, if that school were more fun to go to, attendance would be a lot higher, and the school would be a lot richer,'' I said. I put a forkful of Rice-a-Roni into my mouth and chewed on it for a while. ''I wish I were in charge.''

''I wish you were, too, dear,'' said Mom. ''I'm sure you'd make the world a better place for all of us. Now, please, finish up your dinner. I've made your favorite dessert. It's—''

''Lemon pudding,'' we said simultaneously.

7

WE GET OUR INSTRUCTIONS

Weekdays seem to crawl along like snails, but the weekends tend to clip past like a roadrunner. Usually. The weekend before the board meeting felt like a month. I imagined it must have seemed even longer to Mr. Proctor.

On Monday the vice-principal, Ms. Beatty, called the Youth School Board members into her office and told us what we were supposed to do. There were five of us altogether: Amy Burke, Billy Longpre, Candy Moore, Paul Prentice, and myself.

Ms. Beatty, who always seemed to be dressed in gray, had the kind of creepy thin wrists where all the blood vessels and tendons stuck out like in some anatomy book. And she was as rigid and severe as those veins in her arms. I remembered my dad once describing her as a "real no-nonsense gal."

"Listen carefully," she said, after we'd all gathered around her perfectly ordered desk. "I'm not going to repeat this twice. Do you understand?"

We all nodded.

"After tonight's regular meeting Mr. Brant will swear you in as board members," she said, looking us in the eye, one by one. "Your sole order of business will be to pass a resolution calling on all the students in the district to raise their grades by at least one point during the coming year, and to respect the teachers and administrators of their respective schools."

She showed us a sheet of paper with the ridiculous resolution all written out in fancy calligraphy.

"Carrie, as board president, will read the resolution; one of you should second it, and then you should all vote on it. Do you understand?" she asked again.

All of us nodded once more, except for Paul Prentice, who couldn't resist asking, "How should we vote, yes or no?"

Ms. Beatty shut her eyes. It seemed as if she were counting to herself. We all got quiet, even Paul.

When she opened her eyes and looked up, she said, "You will vote yes. Then your job will be over and you will walk back into the audience. Do you understand?"

"Yes, Ms. Beatty," we mumbled.

"Good," she said. "Now get back to class."

The School Board met at eight o'clock that night in the Madison cafeteria, an old concrete-block room, painted green, that had clearly seen better days. In fact, it was so scrungy, you could have figured out the cafeteria menus for the last three months by just looking at the stains splattered across the floor. Guessing what we'd had that day would have been an absolute snap. The room reeked of spaghetti and meatballs.

I suppose everyone wanted to find out what was going to happen to Mr. Proctor, because by the time we arrived the place was packed. Luckily, there were some empty seats near the back and the three of us settled in.

I was glad that Dad had decided to come, but I wished—just once—that he could have gone somewhere without bringing along his work. We hadn't been seated two minutes when he pulled out his briefcase, yanked out a stack of legal forms, and checked out for the evening.

At ten after eight the five members of the board took their seats at a long table at the far end of the cafeteria. Mr. Brant pounded his gavel for quiet and the meeting was under way. During the flag salute I looked around for Mr. Proctor, but didn't see him anywhere. Mrs. Pride was there, however, and we exchanged smiles and little waves.

Another person I spotted was Jamie. Her costume for the night consisted of a blue bandana, a neon orange dress, and pink-and-black-checked tennis shoes. She was seated on the aisle, alongside her mother, a plump, rosy-cheeked woman with a warm, round face. Jamie's parents had been divorced for the last two years, so Mr. Plufphanger, whom I'd yet to meet, wasn't there. From what I'd heard, however, he was supposed to be a very interesting character, even weirder, some said, than his daughter. Rumor had it that he'd spent a month in jail for causing a riot during Jamie's thirteenth birthday party at a fancy restaurant. I had a feeling he was the source of many of Jamie's crazy stories.

As soon as Jamie saw me wave, she came running over and sat down at my side.

"Bad news," she said. "I turned the library upside down today and I couldn't find that Cocos Island book. Looks like you and I are going to have to trust our memories when we go off after that treasure."

"You and I!" I said. "I never said I was going with you to Cocos Island. Anyway, I'm not so sure that map was real."

"Didn't you see it for yourself?" said Jamie.

"Of course it's real." She gave me a little jab on the arm. "Carrie, look at me. Would I ever steer you wrong?"

Mom shushed us quiet before I could deliver my sarcastic reply.

The meeting dragged on and on. The board discussed and voted on a wide variety of uninteresting things ranging from the amount of money to be spent on a sprinkler system for the elementary school to whether or not Mr. Farnsworth at the high school should be granted a leave. It was nearly ten when Mr. Brant announced the next order of business would be consideration of the continued employment of the junior-high-school librarian, Mr. Samuel Proctor.

There was a stir in the audience and a bunch of people started talking, but they were quickly silenced by Mr. Brant's gavel.

"We have a lot of people who would like to speak to both sides of this issue," said Mr. Brant. "So, please, everyone keep quiet during the proceedings so that we won't be here all night."

For the next hour at least a dozen people marched to the front to speak about Mr. Proctor and the library.

Mr. Corliss spoke first. "Mr. Proctor had ignored repeated warnings from me concerning inappropriate books in the school library," he said. "Though I like Sam personally, I found that in the end I had no choice but to recommend suspension."

Mrs. Burke spoke about the bad language in the books. "Some of it even made me blush," she said. And when someone in the audience shouted out they'd like her to quote some of the offensive passages, she said she just couldn't. "At least not in public," she said, blushing.

Mr. Proctor had his defenders. I'm proud to say that Mrs. Pride gave a wonderful speech about the Bill of Rights, adding, "I've found my students are old enough to choose their own books, and to make up their own minds concerning the merits of the literature they do select."

Three or four parents spoke in support of Mr. Proctor as well.

In the end, however, the decision was left to Mr. Brant and the other four members of the board. Jamie and I grasped hands while each board member was asked for his vote. The board itself split two to two, but the tie was broken by Brant, who voted for Mr. Proctor's dismissal.

For some reason I had always thought Mr. Proctor would get his job back. I had always believed, as in the movies, that all troubles deserved a happy ending. So when the verdict was announced, I felt sick.

And then, when I saw Mr. Proctor himself hurrying out of the cafeteria (I guess he'd been sitting up in front all along), I started to cry.

"Please, dear," said Mom, wrapping her arms around me. "I understand how you feel. I'm upset too. But you've got to stop crying. Remember, you go on next."

I pulled myself out of her arms and wiped my face with my sleeve.

"I don't care about that stupid board," I blubbered. "I just—just want to go home."

"You got to be kidding," said Jamie. "I've sat here for three long, boring hours just to see you up at that table. You leave now and I'll never talk to you again, I swear."

I looked at Jamie and tried to force a smile, but all that came out was a cross between a moan and a sigh.

"Come on," said Jamie. She gave me a little jab in the shoulder. "Get on up there. You can certainly do a better job than Brant. We need you, Carrie. Now more than ever."

I put my finger onto the tip of my nose and thought for a moment about what Jamie had just said. At last, nodding, I said, "Maybe you got something."

"And I got something too," said Mom. She reached down under her seat and came up with a little blue paper bag.

"Something for me?" I asked.

And when Mom pulled a perfect white gardenia out of the bag I gasped and said, "Oh, Mom, you remembered."

"Of course," she said, pinning it onto my dress. "How could I forget?"

I lowered my head and inhaled the delicious smell. Ever since I could remember, Mom had given me a gardenia, my favorite flower, on all special occasions. No birthday, recital, or graduation had slipped by without a gardenia from my mother. In all the excitement about Mr. Proctor I'd forgotten that the night was a special time for me as well. But Mom hadn't forgotten. She never does, and I loved her for it.

I took her hand and thanked her just as Mr. Brant asked for me and the Youth Day School Board to step to the front of the room.

"You're going, aren't you, dear?" asked Mom.

Ever since Jamie's remark a plan had been taking shape in my head. "Of course I'm going," I said. I lowered my head and sniffed the gardenia once again. "How could I miss such a special occasion?"

Jamie gave me another jab on the shoulder and I got to my feet and began edging my way toward the aisle.

"Go get 'em," said Dad as I passed him by.

I nodded. Dad didn't know it at that time, but that was exactly what I'd decided to do—and then some.

HOW TO TAKE
OVER A SCHOOL

The regular board stepped to one side and the five of us took our seats at the table. Everyone clapped. Mrs. Burke took a picture of Amy. Billy Longpre waved to his mom. And I took a series of deep breaths and tried to calm my pounding heart.

Mr. Brant stood in front of the table and read from a proclamation passed earlier by the board.

"Be it known," he began, his voice booming out as if he were the town crier, "that the students seated before you, Carrie Burns, Amy Burke, Candy

Moore, Paul Prentice, and Billy Longpre, have been designated to serve as School Board members in connection with this city's Youth Day festivities. On behalf of the other board members I can tell you that we're proud to give up our seats to this distinguished group of young people." Red-faced, Mr. Brant winked to the audience like a jolly Santa and said, "If the students will please rise, I'd like to administer the official oath of office."

Mr. Brant was acting as if the whole thing were a joke. He must have thought it was cute to make everything so official and legal. That's what everyone must have thought. The fools.

We all rose and Mr. Brant administered a long oath of office in which we promised to fulfill the duties of School Board members and to work for the benefit of all the students and staff of the district.

"I do so swear," we all said.

"May you exercise your powers wisely," said Mr. Brant. Then, handing me the proclamation I'd seen earlier in Ms. Beatty's office, he added, "Carrie Burns, the School Board president, has a resolution she'd like to read and have the new board vote on." He winked again at the audience, and as everyone was clapping, he stepped to the side and folded his arms across his chest.

Shaking, but trying not to show it, I rose to my feet and said, "If it's all right with everyone, I'd like to talk to my new board members for a moment before we vote on the resolution."

Mr. Brant smiled and nodded his approval. "You're the boss," he said.

Everyone gathered around me and I whispered my plans to the newly sworn board members.

"You can't be serious!" gasped Amy.

"I don't know," said Billy.

"Sounds like fun," said Paul. "Count me in."

"Candy?" I said.

She hesitated for a moment, then smiled. "Why not?"

We went back to our seats, and I banged the gavel for order, smoothed down my tan skirt with my free hand, and stood up as straight as I could.

"Ladies and gentleman," I began, "before we vote on the resolution I'd like to first make a motion that the Youth Day School Board become, as of this moment, the permanent School Board, complete with all powers the School Board enjoys."

The motion was seconded by Candy and for a moment the room was dead quiet. Everyone seemed stunned, and maybe a little confused. Then a couple of people laughed and others began talking among themselves. No one seemed to have understood that I was deadly serious, but I quieted them all down with a rap of the gavel and said, "Billy, how do you vote?"

"No," he said.

"Paul?"

"Yes."

"Amy?"

"No!" she said, loud.

"Candy?"

"Yes."

"And I'll break the tie with a yes," I said. "The motion passes."

I drew in a deep breath and without pausing said, "Now, on to the next order of business. I propose that the school district rehire Mr. Samuel Proctor and reopen his library. Do I hear a second?"

"Second!" said Candy, grinning.

I would have pushed on to the vote, but the reality of what I was doing must have finally sunk in, touching off a mixture of boos, shouts, and excited chatter that brought the proceedings to a dead halt. It was like a classroom coming alive when the teacher steps out into the hall. I pounded the gavel for order, but it did no good. Before I could bring it down a second time, Mr. Brant had angrily seized me by the wrist.

"What in the world do you think you're doing?" he said, spitting out the words like venom. "Give me the gavel."

"Let go of my hand," I said, "or I'll scream. I swear."

He released my hand quick enough, but then motioned with his finger for the gavel. "Give it to me, Carrie." Narrowing his ugly eyes, he added, "I plan to have you suspended for this."

Ignoring him now, I pounded the gavel onto the table as if driving in a giant nail. "Order. Will this meeting please come to order!"

Everyone quieted down and I waved Mr. Brant to one side so that I could see the audience.

"We were granted full powers, we were officially sworn in, and we took our seats," I said. My confidence level was on the rise. "The way I see it, we can do whatever we want as long as we try to do our best for the city's schools."

"Why, why . . . this is outrageous!" exploded Mr. Brant. I'd never seen his face so red. He turned to the audience and stretched out his hands. "Are we going to let these kids take over the schools?"

"Throw them out!" someone yelled.

"Order!" I shouted, pounding the table with the gavel. Then, remembering something I'd seen once on a TV show, I cried, "If this meeting doesn't come to order, I'll have the room cleared!"

That stopped everyone for a moment. Long enough, at least, for my father to get out of his seat and walk to the front of the room.

"I'm an attorney," he said loudly, "and I am of the opinion that these kids are legally within their rights. We may learn later that they have over-stepped their bounds, but for now I'm confident that they rightfully hold, with full powers, the seats they occupy on the Madison County School Board."

During the uproar that followed his remarks, my

father took Mr. Brant and the other members of the board over to one side and began explaining the legal basis for his opinion. I restored order with a few bangs of the gavel and called for the board to vote on rehiring Mr. Proctor, which they quickly agreed to do by another three-to-two margin.

After I announced the vote and declared it official, the room once again descended into noisy chaos. Before I could quiet everyone, a stampede of people came charging down the aisle. Some, like Jamie and her mother, were smiling, but others didn't look so friendly, including Mr. Corliss, who came pounding forward like an enraged hippo.

"Carrie Burns," he said, "you've gone too far this time." He puffed himself up and wagged a finger in my face. "As of this moment, young lady, you're suspended."

Buoyed by my father's remarks, I tapped the gavel in the palm of my hand and said, "Mr. Corliss, you can't suspend me, because after tonight I don't think you're going to be principal. As soon as I can restore order I'm going to ask the board to replace you."

Mr. Corliss gasped in shock, but then, jabbing at me with his finger, he said, "You're only making things worse, Carrie."

"I'm serious," I said.

Mr. Corliss sighed. "Even if your board could fire me, which I'm sure they can't, whoever you got to replace me would punish you just the same."

"Not necessarily so," I replied. "Not if I know the person I have in mind for your job."

The principal shook his head and looked down, checking his watch. "If you think Mrs. Pride will let you get away with this, I think you're mistaken."

"I'm not thinking of Mrs. Pride," I said.

"Then who?" asked Mr. Corliss.

I looked to the side and said, "I'm thinking of asking Jamie Plufphanger. I've always thought she had some good ideas of what a school should be."

Mr. Corliss was too stunned to even reply. Three or four people were shouting for my attention. I glanced over and saw my father in heated debate with Mr. Brant. Chaos reigned. Then Candy and Paul, who'd supported me so far, came up and clapped me on the back.

"Hang tough," said Paul.

"Don't worry about that," I said.

"You won't regret your choice," came a familiar voice from over my shoulder.

I turned around. It was Jamie.

"You mean for principal?" I said.

"Yeah." She smiled. "Thanks."

"Put together some ideas and we'll meet at my house in a couple of days," I said. "We're going to make some changes. Aren't we?"

Jamie grinned. "You bet, Carrie. We're going to have us some fun!"

9

I GET FAMOUS

After the meeting a reporter from the Madison
Courier interviewed me, and the story appeared on
page one of the paper the next morning under the
headline LOCAL GIRL SEIZES SCHOOL BOARD. NAMES
FRIEND AS NEW PRINCIPAL OF MADISON JUNIOR HIGH.

It was a terrific story and even featured a picture
of me with my arm around Jamie. It quoted Mr.
Brant as saying he felt the whole thing was ridiculous and that as far as he was concerned Mr. Corliss
was still the principal. He also said that I'd been

temporarily suspended for disrupting the School Board meeting as well as for showing disrespect to the administration. My father was quoted as well, supporting my position and vowing to go to court if necessary to see that the Youth Day board remained in power.

I didn't realize how many people read the Madison *Courier* till the phone began to ring just after breakfast.

"Hello?" I said.

"Carrie Burns?"

"This is Carrie."

"Carrie, this is Susannah Miles of radio station WWDT in Detroit. You're on the air."

"I am!" I exclaimed. I cupped my hand over the receiver. "Mom, Dad, I'm on the radio!"

Ms. Miles wanted to know all about what had happened and what kind of plans I had for the schools now that I was in charge. It was great fun, and so were the next three calls, two from other radio stations and one from *The New York Times*. But by the fourth call, and certainly by the fifth, sixth, seventh, eighth, ninth, and who knows how many others, I was getting tired of mechanically repeating the same story.

I got excited all over again, however, when late in the morning a film crew showed up from CBS and I went outside to be interviewed for *The CBS Evening News*. They talked to my mom and also to my dad, and they said they were planning to interview Mr. Brant a little later.

"They shut down our library and fired our librarian," I said to the CBS reporter. "I just wanted to show our principal that we have rights too."

Turning to the camera, the reporter closed by saying, "Whether these kids will ultimately prevail is probably a matter for the courts to decide, but for now, one thing is clear. Young Carrie Burns and her fellow students are getting an invaluable education in the uses and exercise of law and power here in the United States."

Watching myself that night on TV was unreal. There I was, Carrie Burns, on national television. And when Dan Rather signed off following the story with his traditional "Good night," it was as if he were talking directly to me.

Wow. National TV. I couldn't believe it. By golly, I was famous!

10

PEG-LEG BONES

I think I could have spent the rest of my life giving interviews if I'd wanted. The phone just never stopped ringing. But I had a school district to run, and I had to get down to business. So Wednesday morning I called up everyone on the Youth Day board and asked them to come to my house at noon for a meeting. Then I took the phone off the hook.

Billy said he couldn't come because he didn't want to get into trouble. A likely story. What I suspect really happened was that Amy had gotten to him first. Though she couldn't have cared less about Billy Longpre, he would do anything for her. How he could like her so much was, to me, one of the world's great mysteries. Anyway, the result was that he wasn't coming.

When I phoned Amy her response was simple, and predictable. "I wouldn't come if you paid me a million bucks."

But Jamie came, dressed in a silky thrift-store dress with a pair of mismatched tennis shoes on her feet, and Paul and Candy promised to come as well.

Our school didn't have sports teams, but if it had, Candy would have been a cheerleader. She was blond with a neat little turned-up nose and a ton of freckles. But it wasn't her good looks that made her cheerleader material. It was her positive attitude. She was the sunniest person you'd ever want to meet. I can't remember ever seeing her without a smile. A real original, she was, like an alien from the Planet Happy.

She bounced in through the door and threw her arms around me as if we hadn't seen each other in a hundred years.

"Carrie, I saw you on TV last night. You looked great!" She turned to Jamie. "Isn't this fun!"

Before Jamie could respond, Candy added, "Can you believe it? I've been suspended!"

"Me too," I said. "But we'll be back soon enough. My dad's been working night and day on our case.

He says he's going to have Jamie sitting behind the principal's desk by the end of next week—at the latest."

"Your dad's been working night and day?" said Jamie. "Are you talking about the same guy that used to be too busy to help you with your homework?"

"Same dad," I said. "But ever since the meeting the weirdest thing has happened. Before I took over the School Board he hardly noticed me. In fact, I'm not sure he knew he had a daughter. But now ..." I smiled. "Things have sure changed."

"That's wonderful," said Jamie.

"Believe me," I said, "I'm not complaining."

Just then the doorbell rang. It was Paul, dressed in a GIVE A HOOT—DON'T POLLUTE T-shirt and brown cords that barely reached his ankles. All that was needed to complete his outfit was a neon sign taped to the top of his thick glasses flashing the word NERD. Fortunately, though, Paul wasn't the slightest bit nerdy. He only dressed the way he did for laughs. At least I hoped so.

"Thanks for coming," I said.

"There's not a lot to do when you're suspended," he said.

"You too?" said Candy.

"When Ms. Beatty found out I was at school yesterday she threw a fit," said Paul. "Jamie, soon as you get to be principal, promise me you'll fire her, okay?"

Jamie licked at her lips. "It'll be my pleasure."

"Whoa ... wait a minute," I said. I fixed my eyes on Jamie. "Your job is not to seek revenge, my friend. It's to improve the school. Make it more fun. Remember?"

Jamie snapped her fingers and winked at Paul. "Oh, yeah," she said. "Now I remember."

"Please, Jamie," I said, "please, let's not blow this."

For the next hour or so we sat around the dining-room table and talked about our plans for Madison. We came up with some good ideas, I thought. And a few silly ones too. Paul, for instance, proposed that we reverse the school year, beginning classes in June, then taking nine months off starting in the fall. And Candy's contribution was to suggest a rule allowing everyone to bring pets to school—except for horses, cows, and pigs, she was quick to add.

We might have gone on longer, but the meeting came to a sudden end when Jamie let slip her interest in Cocos Island.

"If I'm principal, I guess Cocos Island is out," she said. "At least for the next year or two."

"Cocos Island?" said Paul. "You mean off the coast of Central America?"

"Yeah," said Jamie. "Near Costa Rica, to be exact. What do you know about it?"

"I know there's a fabulous treasure there," he said. "I read about it in a book."

"Oh," said Jamie. She was trying desperately to be casual. "What kind of a book, Paul?"

"Just an old book I found in the school library. Have you read it too?"

"Uh, no, don't think that I have," she said. She shot me a worried look and I thought I detected a few beads of sweat on her forehead. "You say there's a treasure there?"

"Supposed to be millions," said Paul. "Captain Kidd buried it."

"That so?" said Jamie. She swallowed hard and said, "Sounds interesting. I'll have to look it up."

"It's a terrific book," said Paul. "But when I was reading it I got a little carried away. My mom used to be a librarian and if she ever found out what I did she'd kill me, for sure."

Candy's eyes got round as silver dollars. "What did you do?"

"Promise not to tell?" said Paul.

We nodded and leaned forward.

Paul looked around the room to make sure we were alone, then said, "I wrote in the book. My mom says that's the worst thing you can do."

I looked up and saw Jamie slowly close her eyes. "What did you write?" I asked, even though I already knew the answer.

Paul shook his head slowly, as if remembering some long-ago joke. "Ah," he said, "I scribbled some nonsense on an old map that was in the book. I pretended to be an old pirate spilling out the secret to the treasure. It was just a dumb joke, but I think I really wrecked the map. You guys got to swear you'll never tell my mom.''

''We won't tell,'' I promised.

''Gee, Jamie,'' said Candy, ''did you say you were going there?''

Jamie looked totally spaced. ''Where? The library?''

''Cocos Island,'' said Paul. ''You said something about a trip.''

''Oh, ummmm, yeah,'' said Jamie. ''Cocos Island. Sure. Someday. Just for a vacation, you know. I hear the beaches are really beautiful.''

''Maybe you'll find the treasure,'' said Candy, practically bubbling over with the thought.

''Nah,'' said Jamie. ''I'd just go to get a tan. Treasure really doesn't interest me much.'' She sighed, then added, ''At least not lately, I'm afraid.''

11

MY DAD

Of all the things that happened following the School Board coup, none meant more to me than the changes I saw taking place in my father. He was a different man, happier than I'd ever seen him. Maybe it was because he was working for me full-time instead of putting in his hours for sour-faced Mr. Bodsworth down at the firm. Or maybe it was because of spring, or something that he saw or read. Could have been anything, I suppose. But I do know this: no mean-talking drill sergeant could have made him do a snappier about-face.

His work, which I used to consider just part of the table setting, suddenly disappeared at dinnertime. When someone spoke he listened. And he even spoke too! He carried on regular conversations. He asked what we'd done during the day, and inquired about our health. And, of course, he kept us all posted and up to the minute on everything that was going on regarding the school case. I actually began to like him when I found out who he was. And Mom loved it too. I could tell by the way she looked at him when he talked. And especially when he listened.

The legal maneuvers over the school district were fought out for nearly a week. Jamie and I sat tight and awaited orders. Then Sunday night, not long after I'd turned off my light, Dad came into my room and sat down on the edge of the bed.

"Carrie? Are you still awake?" The light from the full moon streamed through the open curtains and softly lit his face.

"Hi, Dad. What's up?"

"I have some good news," he said. "I just heard from Judge Kennedy. He's issued an injunction forbidding Brant from interfering with your board. It means you're free to take over the schools tomorrow."

I gasped. "Really?"

"Really." He smiled.

Suddenly I was sitting up and my arms were

around my father's neck. "Dad, that's wonderful. Terrific." I gave him a kiss on the cheek and I felt him hug me back. "I can't thank you enough."

He held me out at arm's length and looked into my eyes. "It's you who deserve all the praise, Carrie. I can't begin to tell you how proud you've made me. I just wish I'd noticed it all earlier."

I smiled and thought of how handsome he looked just then. "Some fathers are so busy with their own lives, they never get a chance to see their children growing up," he continued. "Then one day they turn around and their kids are grown ... and gone."

He paused and looked out the window. Turning back to me, he sighed and said, "I've missed out on so much, sweetie."

I saw him swallow hard and thought he might have been crying. I felt a little choked up myself.

He hugged me again and said, "From now on I'm going to make up for things. You'll see."

I hugged him back. "I love you, Dad. Really."

We held each other for a minute or two without saying a word. Then, finally, he patted me on the back and got to his feet. Looking up into his eyes, I could see them sparkling in the moonlight.

"You better be getting some sleep," he said. "You have a big day tomorrow. I do too." Smiling, he bent down, smoothed back my hair, and gave me a kiss on the forehead. "Good night, sweetie. I love you very much."

I felt warm all over. "Good night, Dad."

In the morning I woke up to the most delicious scent in the world. It was as if the whole room had been filled with the sweet smells of a summer's night. I drew in a deep breath, stretched, and sat up. On my nightstand I discovered a note in my father's hand which read: *To the most wonderful daughter in the world. Good luck on your big day.* Next to the note was a silver bowl, and floating in the bowl was a perfect white gardenia.

12

LOBSTER IN
THE RAIN

After breakfast I called up Jamie and the other board members and told them to come to school at one that afternoon. Candy and Paul were thrilled when I told them the news, but Jamie wasn't the least bit excited.

"What's wrong?" I asked. "Isn't this what we've been waiting for?"

"Yeah, sure. I suppose," she said. "It's just that I've been thinking. Maybe everyone is right. I'm only thirteen. What do I know about being a principal?''

"Jamie," I said, "you can't quit now. If you do, everything we fought for will be lost."

"Carrie, I'm an eighth grader," she argued. "I should be out running around, not sitting in a stuffy office setting educational goals and lecturing kids for cutting classes."

"Wait a minute," I said. "Do you think I want to sit in School Board meetings all next year? Of course not, but we have to do this for Mr. Proctor and Mrs. Pride and for everyone else at that sorry school. Don't you see? We have to!''

There was a long pause at the other end of the line. Finally, Jamie said, "You don't think we've made our point?''

"Jamie, don't you remember what Eric said in class?''

"No, what?''

"He said the only way to get the administration's attention is with an ax. Jamie, today at one you've got to be that ax.''

"I do?" she said.

"You do," I replied. "See you this afternoon."

"One o'clock?''

"Yes, one o'clock," I repeated.

The morning had been clear, but by noontime a storm had moved in and the skies above town were heavy with thick gray clouds, their undersides billowing and rolling and looking to burst like swollen balloons.

I was afraid that the threat of rain might have kept everyone home, but when Mom and Dad and I drove up to Madison at one, I saw that I couldn't have been more wrong. Besides Candy, Paul, and Jamie there must have been at least a dozen reporters and TV cameramen standing near the steps to the school, as well as twenty or more parents and relatives, most of whom I didn't recognize. Up on the steps themselves, arrayed like soldiers defending their castle, were Mr. Brant and Mr. Corliss. Slightly behind the two old warriors stood Mrs. Pride and three other teachers, and behind them was a whole bunch of students, including Amy Burke in a spotless white skirt and pink blouse.

Jamie, Candy, and Paul came up to us when we got out of the car and said hello nervously.

"Everybody ready?" asked Dad.

"Yes, sir, Mr. Burns," said Candy.

"Well, then, let's go," said Dad, and we proceeded to make our way through the crowd and up the steps to where Mr. Brant was standing, red-faced and stiff as a frozen lobster.

Handing Mr. Brant a sheet of paper, Dad said, "Last night Judge Kennedy issued this injunction enjoining you or your staff from interfering with Jamie Plufphanger, who today plans to assume the principal's post currently being filled by Mr. Milton Corliss."

Mr. Brant read the document and then handed it back to my father. "I'm not sure this is valid," he said. "It's in considerable error."

A low, distant roll of thunder swept over the school, but my father didn't seem to take the slightest notice. "Error?" he said. "Just what are you referring to?"

Mr. Brant glanced over at Mr. Corliss. "It says the office being occupied by Milton Corliss. Well, Mr. Corliss is no longer principal here. He's been promoted to assistant superintendent in charge of grounds and facilities."

"I don't understand," said my father.

"Following all the publicity in the media, as well as remarks parents, teachers, and others have made to me personally, I felt I had no choice but to relieve Mr. Corliss of his administrative educational duties. Clearly, he'd lost the confidence of the community."

"You've probably made a wise decision," said my father. "Nevertheless, the injunction is still valid." He put one hand on Jamie's shoulder and another on mine. "Ladies, shall we proceed?"

Mr. Brant took a step backward and thrust out his hand as if he were a traffic cop in a third-grade reader. "Wait, wait," he said. "Are you sure you're doing the right thing? Miss Plufphanger may have some wonderful ideas. I don't dispute that. But do you really think she's capable of serving as principal of a major junior high school?"

I looked over at Mrs. Pride and saw her smile. I
smiled back.

"Perhaps," said Mr. Brant, somewhat desperately,
"perhaps we can arrange a compromise."

I looked up at Dad then back to Mr. Brant. "What
kind of a compromise?" I asked.

I heard another crack of thunder, this one closer.
Mr. Brant looked over his shoulder to make sure he
wasn't about to be swept away by the storm, then
said, "If Carrie will give me my job back, and if
Jamie will resign, then I promise you the school
board will let the two of you select the new principal."

I looked over at Jamie and raised my eyebrows.
"Could we pick anybody?" asked Jamie.

"Anybody as long as they are academically qualified," said Mr. Brant. "I'm sure you could find
someone who'll carry out your educational ideas. I
won't try to influence you one bit."

I looked up at Dad and asked him what he thought.
"It sounds fair," he said. "But the final decision
has to be up to you, Jamie and your board."

I looked to Candy and Paul and they answered
with a shrug of their shoulders. I felt just as confused. The crowd edged forward, pressing in close to
hear my decision. Almost instinctively I looked over
to Mrs. Pride for help, and saw her make the "Okay"
sign with her thumb and first finger.

The wind picked up and with it came the smell of
the approaching storm.

"I'm making a fair offer," said Mr. Brant. "What do you say?"

"What about Mr. Proctor?" I asked.

"He was reinstated this morning," said Mr. Brant. "He'll be back at work tomorrow."

I'd never seen Mr. Brant so cowed. He seemed desperate to get his job back, and that piece of paper from Judge Kennedy must have been some serious stuff. I decided to lean on the old goat for at least a few more minutes and see what else I might be able to squeeze out of him.

"What about the books in the library?" I asked.

"Returned last week," he said.

"And what about an apology for Mr. Proctor?"

Mr. Brant shut his eyes and drew in a deep breath. "He'll get one this afternoon. Now, Miss Burns, Miss Plufphanger, do we have a deal?"

I turned again to Dad, and so did Jamie. "Not every court may be as sympathetic as Judge Kennedy's," he said. "And I think you need to keep in mind what would be best for the school."

During all this I'd been noticing Amy Burke edging her way up behind Mr. Brant. I figured she wanted to get in her two cents' worth, and as it turned out, I was right.

"Please," she said, suddenly emerging from behind Mr. Brant, "don't cause any more trouble." She batted her eyes at Mr. Brant as if to say, *Let me speak to these bozos. I'll handle them for you.*

Mr. Brant looked none too happy to have Amy there, but he didn't say anything to stop her, so she put her mouth in gear once again and said, ''We've got to use our heads, gang. Take Mr. Brant's offer and we can all be happy again. What do you say?''

Jamie wrinkled her nose and dismissed Amy with a wave of her hand. ''Come on, Amy,'' she said. ''Don't make me barf.''

Amy's mouth dropped open just as a great crack of thunder exploded above us like a cannon shot. We all froze for a moment, then Amy collected herself and said, ''If Jamie is made principal, Madison will, be the laughingstock of the city.'' She took a step my way and held out her hands at arm's length, palms up. ''Carrie, please, you're a sensible girl. Do what's best for Madison.''

''Amy,'' said Jamie, ''why don't you just butt out?''

Amy gasped, then nearly staggered backward. ''Why—why, Jamie, why don't you just—just—'' Unable to find the words, she finally stomped her foot and began coming at Jamie.

Jamie took a step forward as well, and Mr. Brant thrust out his arms. ''Girls, girls, please!''

Jamie glared at Amy, then set her jaw and said, ''I'm ready to go now . . . to the principal's office.''

Mr. Brant was flabbergasted. ''You're not serious,'' he said. ''But what about the deal?''

''Jamie,'' I said, confused, ''are you sure this is the right thing to do?''

"Jamie, you're just being plain stupid," said Amy.

I felt a drop of rain, then another and another.

"Ms. Burke!" said Jamie. "I'm the principal now, and you'd better start showing me some respect."

"I'll show it when you earn it," responded Amy.

"I don't have to take this," said Jamie. "Report to my office at once!"

Suddenly there was a another, tremendous clap of thunder and the skies opened up. The cameramen and reporters quickly gathered their equipment and scurried for cover.

Amy squealed and tried to protect her precious hair with her hands as she ran up the steps into the school.

"Amy!" shouted Jamie, catching up to her just before she could duck into a classroom. "Didn't you hear what I said? I want you in my office! And I want you there now."

13

ON THE JOB

Jamie threw open the door to the office, catching Mrs. Omani in the middle of applying a layer of powder to her bright red cheeks.

"Amy!" shouted Jamie, extending her arm toward the principal's office. "Inside!"

Mrs. Omani hastily folded up her compact and sprang to her feet. "Whoa! Hey! Jamie! Where do you think you're going?"

Jamie paused and studied the secretary with contempt. "My dear Mrs. Omani," she sniffed, "if you don't mind, I'm going into my office." She raised an eyebrow. "That's all right, isn't it?"

Mrs. Omani sank back into her chair. "Spare me, please. Are you really the new principal?"

Amy and I nodded, and Jamie just smiled.

"Unbelievable," Mrs. Omani muttered, shaking her head. "Heavens, what have I done to deserve this?"

Jamie opened the door to the office and ushered me and Amy inside.

"Oh, Mrs. Omani," she said, "from now on I'd appreciate it if you wouldn't use my first name. It's Ms. Plufphanger."

Through the open door I could see Mrs. Omani roll her eyes.

Jamie shut the door, then opened it a second later to add, "And one more thing."

"What is it now?" asked Mrs. Omani wearily.

Jamie smiled. "I'm going to be busy for a while with Amy and I don't want to be disturbed. So, please, hold all my calls."

I thought I heard Mrs. Omani growl just as Jamie shut the door once again.

Jamie motioned for Amy and me to sit down, and we did, in hard-backed wooden chairs in front of Mr. Corliss's perfectly ordered desk.

"So," said Jamie, plopping down in Mr. Corliss's chair, "what are we going to do with you, Amy?"

Amy looked a little jittery, but I could see she was trying her best not to show it.

"What do you mean?" she asked.

"I mean we can't very well have students running around calling the principal stupid, can we?" said Jamie.

"Come on, Jamie," said Amy, "I didn't even know you were going to be principal."

"That's no excuse!" she shouted, slamming her fist onto the desk with such force that a pile of papers leapt an inch. "You have to learn some respect. You're suspended a week."

"What? What?" blubbered Amy.

"You heard me . . . now, get out or I'll make it for a month."

"But, Jamie," protested Amy, "I thought we were—"

"Out . . . out!" shouted Jamie, pointing to the door. "I don't want to hear any more of your back talk. I'm principal now, and I don't have to take it."

Amy got to her feet and shuffled to the door. Just before she went out she turned around, eyes filled with tears, and said, "Jamie Plufphanger, you're— you're just as bad as Mr. Corliss." She started to cry. She caught her breath, then shouted, "Maybe even worse!" Then she turned and went out, slamming the door behind her.

As soon as she was gone, Jamie put her feet up on the desk and her hands behind her head. "Hey, being principal is more fun than I thought," she said. "Who shall we call in next? What about the science teacher, Mr. Dawson? He gave me a D last year. I think I'll cut his salary in half. What do you think?"

"I don't think very much of it at all," I said. "Jamie, I didn't appoint you principal so that you could go on the rampage against your old enemies." I shook my head. "You're supposed to be above that."

"Carrie, baby," said Jamie. "Hey, can't we have a little fun?"

"Frankly, no," I said, getting up. "We've got to get this school reorganized. Isn't that why we've gone to all this trouble?"

Just then there was a knock at the door.

"Who is it?"

"It's me," said Mrs. Omani. "Your schedule's ready."

Jamie gave me a quizzical look. "Schedule?" she said. "Come in!"

Mrs. Omani opened the door and walked in stiffly. She dropped a sheet of paper on the desk in front of Jamie and said, "This is your weekly schedule. As you'll note, you are due to address the Kiwanis Club tomorrow at noon. Since you don't drive, you'll have to find someone to take you there. Be sure to be back by three, when Mr. Chambers will be here to discuss the problems we're having with the boiler. Mrs. Burke and the PTA want to see you also, so I'll try to crowd them in before five. Then there's the—"

"Before five ... you mean five in the afternoon?" asked Jamie.

"We all work here until five," said Mrs. Omani. "Mr. Corliss, in fact, often stayed later, or took work home because—"

"But school's out at three," said Jamie.

Mrs. Omani smiled and said sarcastically, "But you're not a student anymore, Ms. Plufphanger. You're a principal of a very busy, very large school. And you have obligations, and commitments, and duties and—"

"Enough! Enough!" said Jamie, waving a hand in her face. "I'll look over the schedule this afternoon and see if it's all necessary."

Mrs. Omani shook her head. "Believe me, it's all necessary," she said. "Do you want me to try to find you the ride to the Kiwanis Club?"

Jamie absentmindedly shoved the paper to one side. "Oh, I suppose, Mrs. Omani. Do whatever you have to do." She took a deep breath, then sighed and turned to me. "Do you think every day is this bad?"

Mrs. Omani bent down over the desk till she was practically in Jamie's face. "Most days, Ms. Plufphanger, are much, much worse."

14

NEWBERGER'S CHEESE FOOD

I just saw Jamie once during the next four days, and then only for a few seconds. As it happened, I had just come out of math class when I spotted her striding down the hall, a stack of papers a foot thick in her arms, a red bandana on her head, and sequined socks disappearing into mismatched sneakers.

"Jamie, got a minute?"

She paused and gave me a smile. "Sorry, Carrie." She glanced down at the stack of papers in her arms. "I got a zillion things to do, really."

"Maybe we can meet after school," I asked.

"Yeah, maybe then," she said without much conviction. "I'll be in touch."

But we never got together and I didn't hear from her again until Friday in the middle of Mrs. Pride's class, at exactly one forty-six in the afternoon. I knew the time precisely because Jamie chose to communicate via the school intercom, a device which happened to be located just to the left of the room's big chrome clock.

"Hello, out there in Madison land, it's me, Jamie Plufphanger, your illustrious principal," she began immodestly. "Fire up your taste buds, students, because guess who's coming to school ... Mrs. Sweet's chocolate chip cookies! That's right. From now on you won't have to go all the way to the mall to buy Mrs. Sweet's, because starting Monday they'll be available right here in our own cafeteria!" There was a short pause and I pictured her sitting before the microphone, drinking in the imaginary applause. "As of today," she crowed, "Mrs. Sweet's will be known as the official snack food of Madison Junior High."

I'd listened to tons of announcements over the loudspeakers, but I'd never heard one with a commercial before. I wondered what kind of a deal Jamie had signed with Mrs. Sweet's. It didn't sound proper. And maybe it wasn't even legal.

I guess the rest of the class wasn't nearly as worried about it as I was, by the way they were all licking their lips. Even Paul Prentice. Leaning across the aisle, he whispered, "Hey, the new prince is okay, don't you think?"

Before I could reply, Jamie said, "But, friends, that's not all. Starting next week you can kiss your seventh-period classes good-bye, because as of Monday they are officially abolished."

"What?" gasped Mrs. Pride.

"And what," bragged Jamie, "do you imagine your nice new principal will replace those classes with? Study hall? Dumb assemblies? Playground sports? No way. Get this! Instead of classes we're going to have movies! Good ones too. Next Monday, for instance, everybody who doesn't want to go to study hall can come to the auditorium and see *The Miracle Worker*, starring Patty Duke."

I could have guessed. *The Miracle Worker*, a real tearjerker about Helen Keller, was Jamie's all-time favorite movie.

Paul wiggled his eyebrows. "Tell me that girl doesn't know what she's doing. Huh?"

But he changed his tune a second later when Jamie added, "Charge for the film will be just one dollar."

Everyone groaned. After all, Mrs. Pride's seventh-period literature class wasn't costing us a cent. Going to the movies all next week was going to cost us five bucks.

"Enjoy your weekend," she then said, signing

off. "And I'll catch you all next week, same channel, same intercom."

The loudspeaker fell silent, and for a moment the room was perfectly still. Everyone seemed stunned. Finally, Mrs. Pride's voice broke the quiet. "Tell me, did I really hear correctly? No more seventh period? A movie house in the auditorium?" She shook her head and smiled. "An official cookie in the cafeteria?" She glanced up at the loudspeaker, then back at the class. "I hate to say it, but in my opinion I think our illustrious principal has just flipped her wig."

"Flipped her what?" whispered Paul.

"Gone nuts," I whispered back. "Paul, after class we've got to go see Jamie."

"Great idea," he replied. "Get there early so we can check out those sample cookies she's probably got stashed."

I rolled my eyes and tapped my fingers on my desk. "We're not going there for cookies, Paul."

"Oh?" said Paul, pretending ignorance.

"We're going there as School Board members," I said. "To find out just what's going on. Okay?"

Paul winked. "Sure, Carrie. After all, you're the boss."

By the time Paul and I got to the principal's office, it was nearly three. We found Mrs. Omani standing by the door, talking to a bushy-haired fat man wearing a tight blue jacket and red bow tie.

"Here," I heard him say as he thrust a small yellow box at Mrs. Omani. "Treat yourself to a free sample of Newberger's powdered health-food cheese food."

Mrs. Omani took it between two fingers, as if it were crawling with bugs.

"This is health food?" she said.

"As healthy as sunshine and fresh air," he boasted. Lowering his voice, he added. "And a lot cheaper than the cheese you've been serving. Ms. Plufphanger is going to be saving this school a bundle."

"I hope the kids like it," said Mrs. Omani. She looked skeptical.

The salesman hitched up his pants and headed out the door. "They'd better like it," he said. "Starting today it's the official cheese food of Madison Junior High."

We stepped aside and watched till he had waddled away. Mrs. Omani carried the sample back inside and dropped it into the wastebasket. "Health food, my eye!" she sneered. "That man ought to be thrown in jail. I don't care how much the school saves. Humph, I bet there's more nutrition in the cardboard box than in the stuff inside."

I nodded sympathetically, then said, "Paul and I need to talk to Jamie. Is she in?"

"It depends," said Mrs. Omani. She sat down at her desk. "What do you have to sell?"

"Nothing," I said. "Common sense, perhaps."

"Jamie could certainly use a bit of that," said
Mrs. Omani. She shook her head. "Would you believe it, Carrie, that Newberger fellow was the fifth
salesman in here today. The fifth! And every one of
them sold her something. According to my count this
school's now got an official chocolate chip cookie, an
official cheese food, and even an official potato chip.
And yesterday we became the first junior high to
have an authorized tennis shoe, and starting next
month she's scheduled a series of weekend rock concerts for the auditorium." Mrs. Omani put her hand
to the side of her face. "You wouldn't believe the
fellow that sold her the concerts. He had pink-and-
orange hair and—and a paper clip through his nose!"
She shut her eyes and tried to put the thought out of
her head. "Frankly, Carrie, I think she's flipped her
wig."

"That sounds familiar," said Paul.

"Well, it's true," said Mrs. Omani. She picked up
the phone and pushed down one of the buttons.
"Don't be surprised if she won't see you."

"She'll see me," I said. "She better. I gave her
the job."

"It's Paul Prentice and Carrie Burns," said Mrs.
Omani. "Can I send them in?"

There was a long pause, then Mrs. Omani looked
up and placed her hand over the receiver. "She says
sorry but she's impossibly busy. She wants to know
if Monday afternoon at one would be okay."

I narrowed my eyes. "It certainly would not be okay!" I looked up at the clock. It read two-fifteen. "Tell Jamie that her two-fifteen appointment is here."

Before Mrs. Omani could utter a reply, I stepped to the door and threw it open, catching the principal behind her desk, the phone still in her hand.

"Jamie Plufphanger, I want to talk to you—now!" I stomped into the room with Paul close behind and stood in front of her desk. "Tell me, Ms. Illustrious Principal, since when have best friends needed appointments to see each other?"

Jamie smiled weakly and hung up the phone. I'd never seen a desk as messy as the one she sat behind. There must have been half a foot of papers piled on it, some of them no more than crumpled-up balls, as if a trash truck had just backed up and unloaded.

Paul surveyed the desk with considerable wonder. "Is this all stuff you're supposed to do?"

"Supposed to," sighed Jamie. "Only trouble is, none of it makes any sense to me." She reached into the mess and held out a yellow sheet of paper covered with numbers. "These are the estimates for the new boiler the school needs. Can you figure it out?"

Paul shrugged his shoulders and Jamie let it flutter back to the desk. "And look at this," she said, digging out a two-page letter sporting a fancy letterhead. "Someone wants to know if our English department employs something called Bloom's taxonomy, and if it incorporates performance-based objectives." She slipped it back into the pile. "I mean, give me a break!"

She let out a long sigh and waved her hand at the desk. "Another week in this job and I'm going to be buried under paper. It just never seems to stop." She smiled. "Maybe now you can understand why I can't afford to take out time for gossip."

"We didn't come to gossip," said Paul. "We came to talk about that dumb movie festival of yours."

"Dumb? You calling the story of Helen Keller dumb?"

"Jamie, I'm sure that—"

"What? What are you telling me, Paul? That you don't like Helen Keller? Is that it?"

"Jamie," said Paul, "the point isn't the movie. It's that you can't charge a dollar for seventh period."

"Well, what can I charge?" she asked. "The movies are cheap, but we're not getting them for free."

I pointed out that school was supposed to be free. "You can't make money off the students," I said.

"Well, then, just where am I going to make it?" asked Jamie. "Carrie, do you remember how Corliss used to complain about the school not having any money? Well, I've found out he was right."

"But, Jamie," I said, grinning. "Really, an official cheese food? Authorized tennis shoes? Come, now. I get the impression you've been doing nothing but thinking up get-rich-quick schemes."

She flashed me that big exaggerated smile of hers. "Not much else I could do." She waved again at the mound of paperwork topping her desk. "Everything else about this job is as mysterious as an Egyptian tomb. What do you think I should do? Sit around all day and twiddle my toes?"

Jamie had a point. Of course, I should have seen it all earlier. Plufphanger, after all, was the get-rich-quick queen of Madison, maybe of the whole universe. She was only doing what came naturally, and the fact that her obsession was harming the school was but an unfortunate side effect.

"You know, I don't think Mrs. Pride likes your plans for getting rid of seventh period," said Paul.

Jamie winced. "Was she mad?"

"A little, I think," I said.

She winced again. "I hate making her mad, but what can I do?" She looked to me for sympathy. "You know, I'm going to have to lay her off. The language teachers too."

"Jamie!" I gasped. "You can't be serious."

"I really have no choice," she said. "And I'm afraid the PE department has to go too. This school simply can't afford the insurance."

I felt my face redden. "I don't believe you, Jamie Plufphanger. Our plan for the school was to add classes, not cut them!"

"It's only temporary," she said. "Just till we get through the next few months. Then we can put everything back, and then some. We have to be realistic. Laying those teachers off is going to save the school a hundred thousand dollars, at least.''

''But—but you just can't fire everyone who—''

''Carrie, I told you. It's only temporary. Just until we see how the rock concerts do, and how much we can save in the cafeteria.''

''You mean how much we can make,'' I said. It was everything I could do to contain my temper. ''I'm beginning to wonder if maybe the old board wasn't right. An eighth grader can't run a school.''

Jamie leaned over the papers and held out her hands. ''You think this job is easy, huh? Know what I have to do this afternoon? Go downstairs and look at the boiler with a salesman from Turner Plumbing. Then after that I've got to settle a fight between Mrs. Gaines and Mr. Farnsworth over smoking in the teachers' lounge.'' She drew in a deep breath. ''And tomorrow I'm supposed to speak to the Elks Club downtown. And I don't even know where the meeting is, or how I'm going to get there. Probably have to ride my bike. A bike! A principal shouldn't be pedaling a bicycle, she should be riding in a limousine.''

''Limousine? Jamie, you have gone money crazy.'' I took Paul by the arm. ''Come on. Let's get out of here before she tries to sell us some cookies, or shoes or—''

''Carrie, please . . .''

I turned around at the door and aimed a finger at the principal. "Jamie Plufphanger, I'm warning you. You'd better not mess with Mrs. Pride's job. Not one little bit."

"Is that so," said Jamie.

"That's so," I said. "You lay off Mrs. Pride or I'll see to it that the School Board lays you off— permanently." I shook my finger for emphasis. "And I'm not kidding either."

Jamie stood up and held out her hands, palms out. "I'm only trying to make a little money for the school." She shook her head. "Paul, you understand, don't you?"

Paul shrugged his shoulders. "Umm, Jamie, I was wondering ..."

Jamie smiled. "Yes, Paul. What is it?"

"Did you get any free cookies from Mrs. Sweet's?"

"Paul!" I said.

"No, sorry, I didn't," said Jamie.

"Oh, I see," said Paul. "Just curious."

"Come on," I said. I took Paul by the arm. "Let's get out of here. This office always did give me the creeps."

I shut the door behind me, but Jamie's shouts followed me down the hall. "I can have you suspended, Carrie Burns. I can, I can. I'm the principal here. Don't you forget that, Carrie!"

15

MIRACLES AND OTHER DISASTERS

Over the weekend word must have leaked out that Jamie was plotting to carve up the language, the PE, and the literature departments, because on Monday morning a crowd of teachers and students clustered outside her office, and they didn't sound too happy. Actually, they sounded like the tower of Babel.

"*¡Usted hace mal a la escuela!*" cried Señor Sánchez.

"*Vous détruisez l'école!*" shouted Madame Klein in French.

And Herr Franken, stomping his foot, his fat nose turning purple, kept repeating, *"Studenten müssen Deutsch lernen!* They must!''

I pushed myself up against the wall and watched the scene unfold. It wasn't until I'd been there a minute that I realized Jamie was in the middle of the whole mess, trying ineffectively to get in a few words of her own, in English.

"Quiero una principal nueva," cried Señor Sánchez. *"¡Por favor!"*

"¡Sí! ¡Sí!" said the Spanish students.

"Oui! Oui!" agreed the French students.

"Deutsch! We must have *Deutsch* !'' said Herr Franken once again.

''Please, please,'' begged Jamie. Her bandana had slipped halfway off her head. If the scene had been played out a hundred years earlier, in the Old West, I'm certain someone would have been sent for a rope.

I didn't think things could get much worse. But that was before I saw the school cook, Mrs. Hanratty, come charging down the hallway, a frying pan in one hand, a box of Newberger's cheese food in the other. Mrs. Hanratty was big, six foot one, and two hundred pounds, and she was mean too. She was the one person at Madison you knew not to cross. I remember one time in the lunch line when I, without thinking, groaned at the sight of a mess of creamed corn she'd just plopped onto my plate. I realized my mistake too late. By then Mrs. Hanratty had already formed her big black eyebrows into a sharp V and was letting me have it.

"You're going to eat it! And you're going to like it, young lady, do you understand?" she barked.

I understood. I nodded and shuffled off down the line before the tirade could continue. You had to move fast once she started, or she'd have you in tears for the rest of the day.

Now everyone was scattering before her like leaves in the wind. I pressed myself deeper into the wall as she barged into the crowd, elbowing aside everyone in her path.

For a moment there was silence. I had my eye on that frying pan. But in the end it was the yellow carton of cheese food that she chose to wave in Jamie's face.

"Did you order this?" she demanded.

Jamie was speechless.

"Someone delivered sixty cases of this junk over the weekend, and now it's all I've got to serve for lunch. Tell me, Miss Plufphanger, what am I going to give the kids for lunch?"

"Cartons of cheese food?" suggested Jamie.

Mrs. Hanratty gave Jamie a withering stare. "Have you taken the time to read what they put in this—this garbage?"

"No, but—"

Mrs. Hanratty raised the frying pan, and the crowd

fell back. "Jamie Plufphanger, you be in the cafeteria at lunch today. The students are going to be eating pizza—and you will be, too, do you understand?"

Jamie nodded and stepped backward toward her office.

"Did I make myself perfectly clear?" she asked.

"Yes, Mrs. Hanratty," said Jamie. "I'll be in the cafeteria at noon."

"You do that," said Mrs. Hanratty. Then, wheeling about, she waved the frying pan in our faces and added, "What are you all staring at? Classes are about to start." She waved the pan again. "Everybody go. Scat!"

By the time lunch rolled around, everyone in school had heard what had happened between Jamie and Mrs. Hanratty. Needless to say, at noon the cafeteria was jammed. The whole student body, and most of the teachers, had turned out in hopes of seeing the two battle again. But when Paul and I got there, Mrs. Hanratty was the only combatant in sight. I pictured Jamie back at the office, huddled behind her desk, the door double-locked.

There was a strange smell hovering over the cafeteria, something akin to the odors that sometimes arise on a hot day behind Henry's Stop 'n' Go Handymart, but for some reason I didn't connect it with the meal being served that afternoon. That was my first mistake. The second one was getting in line.

And the third was when I permitted Mrs. Hanratty to actually serve me the lunch.

"Sorry, Carrie," she said, handing me a plate bearing a single slice of pizza. "It was the best I could do—under the circumstances."

In my two years at Madison I had never heard Mrs. Hanratty apologize for anything, especially her food. It was definitely a bad sign.

A worse sign, however, was the sight of the pizza itself. It was certainly unlike anything I'd ever been served before. For one thing, I'd never seen cheese looking quite like the stuff that was sitting atop my lunch. Instead of melting out smoothly, like lava, this stuff had formed up into tiny little balls the size of BB's. Worse, though, was its color, one of the ugliest shades of green I'd ever seen. It looked like someone had ... I can't say it. There was no way I was going to eat that mess. Nor was Paul. Nor was anyone else in the cafeteria.

Everyone was pinning the blame on Jamie. And Paul showed me why. "Look at how Mrs. Hanratty has advertised lunch," he said, pointing up to the cracked yellow letters on the sign above the cash register. "No wonder everyone's upset."

The sign said: PIZZA À LA PLUFPHANGER. MADE EXCLUSIVELY WITH NEWBERGER'S CHEESE FOOD. THE OFFICIAL CHEESE FOOD OF MADISON.

People were not only angry, they were hungry too. There was nothing else to eat in the whole place but

Mrs. Sweet's chocolate chip cookies, which would hardly be enough for lunch. And besides, they were priced fifty cents higher than the ones at the mall.

Jamie walked into the cafeteria. And that's when the riot started.

Maybe *riot* is too strong a word. *Food fight* would have been more like it. Poor Jamie. No circus clown ever had to endure so many thrown pies. They weren't tasty cream pies either. They were green pizza pies. Last I saw of her, she was tearing off for her office, a pizza slice on her head, another sliding down the back of her dress, and about twenty kids in hot pursuit.

Poor Jamie. Her troubles weren't over yet.

Sometime between lunch and seventh period she acquired a new dress and a fresh bandana. Determined to rescue the day, she next appeared before a large crowd that had paid a dollar a head to see the Madison premiere of the film *The Miracle Worker*. She strode proudly onto the low stage, past the worn piano and the faded flags, and stood in front of the big white screen lowered especially for the afternoon's show.

She waited patiently for the boos and jeers to die away. The pizza lunch, after all, was still fresh in everyone's mind. Then she launched into a brief description of the film, which most everyone already knew was a telling of the early days of the deaf and blind child Helen Keller.

She hadn't gone far when the heckling began. A seventh grader toward the back of the room started things off with a comment to the effect that "we ought to cut the lecturing and start the projectoring."

This encouraged a battalion of others to leap in with such remarks as "We paid for it, let's see it," "On with the show!" and finally, "Beat it, Plufphanger. Off the stage!"

Stunned, Jamie clutched nervously at her dress and endured the taunts. Finally, a boy in the front row yelled for someone to "hit the lights!" And, mercifully, someone did.

Moments later, when the film flickered on, the stage was bare save for the piano, the flags, and the screen. I imagined Jamie backstage, in tears, and knew I had to go to her. We were, after all, still friends—I hoped.

While I was studying the shortest route to the aisle, the room suddenly erupted in a new round of jeers and boos. At first I thought that Jamie had walked back onstage, but I soon discovered that everyone was yelling about her movie. As the music and the titles on the screen revealed, it was not *The Miracle Worker* but, instead, *Miracle on 34th Street.* Even though they both had the word *miracle* in their titles, they had nothing else in common. *Miracle on 34th Street* was an old black-and-white movie about a Santa Claus at Macy's department store. It was a fine film, I'm sure, but who wanted to hear about Christmas in May, and besides, everyone had paid to see something else.

Another riot was in the making. The auditorium was in an uproar. Someone turned on the lights and the audience calmed down long enough for Jamie to walk back onto the stage.

Her appearance didn't exactly settle everyone down, but her promise to refund everyone's money was greeted with applause, the first she'd received that day.

As I later learned, Jamie had ordered the film on the same day she was to speak at the Thirty-fourth Street YMCA. Thinking more of her speech than the movies, she'd mixed up the titles. And the school, instead of making a fortune on the Plufphanger Film Festival, had ended up losing a bundle.

All in all it had not been one of Jamie's better days.

16

THE MADISON PEACE TREATY

I've got to give Jamie credit. Despite Monday's disasters she almost lasted out the week. In the end what finished her off wasn't the lunches, the movies, or the food fights. It was the little things, like the chipped beef she was forced to eat at the Kiwanis Club, the talk with the boiler salesman about pressure valves and noncorrosive piping, and the whole afternoon she spent listening to Mr. Farnsworth and Mrs. Gaines slug it out over smokers' rights in the teachers' lounge.

When I stopped by to see her Thursday she looked as if she'd aged about twenty years. "Another week in this job and I'll have to be put in a rest home," she said.

"Another week in this job and you'll put the school in an insane asylum," I told her.

I gave my friend a long, hard look, then sighed. "You've got to give it up, you know."

"Believe me, it would be my greatest pleasure," said Jamie. "But—but how? I can't just quit and walk away. That's not my style."

I rubbed my chin for a moment and thought. "You wouldn't be quitting if you accepted Brant's offer, you know."

"Interesting idea," said Jamie. "You think it's still open?"

"Wouldn't hurt to give him a call," I said.

Sure enough, when we called he agreed to honor the terms he'd offered us earlier.

"We get to pick the principal?" Jamie said.

She smiled at the reply, then asked, "And there will be no further trouble at the library?"

Jamie cupped her hand over the mouthpiece. "He says if we'll just step down, we can have whatever we want. Shall I ask him for another month off in the summer?"

I laughed. "Just tell him to meet us here tomorrow morning. I'll have my dad bring some papers for him to sign so it will be official."

So, at nine o'clock the next morning my father presided over the signing of what has come to be known as the Madison School Peace Treaty. Immediately after we'd put our signatures on the paper Jamie and I resigned our jobs. But there was no doubt we'd left our marks on the school. In the fall there would be a new principal at Madison and a new academic program as well.

As for Mr. Corliss, he seemed to be enjoying his job supervising the school's maintenance staff, and Mr. Proctor, under our protection, bought more books for the library.

And as for Amy and Jamie, well, they're still fighting. The latest dispute involves the Burkes' new car. Amy was understandably proud of the fancy Corvette her father had recently bought at Sam Davidson's Used Cars, till Jamie started spreading the rumor that the Burkes had just become owners of the infamous Death Car.

"You take it back!" Amy had said.

And Jamie had replied, "Sorry, Amy, but all I'm doing is passing on the news."

As usual.

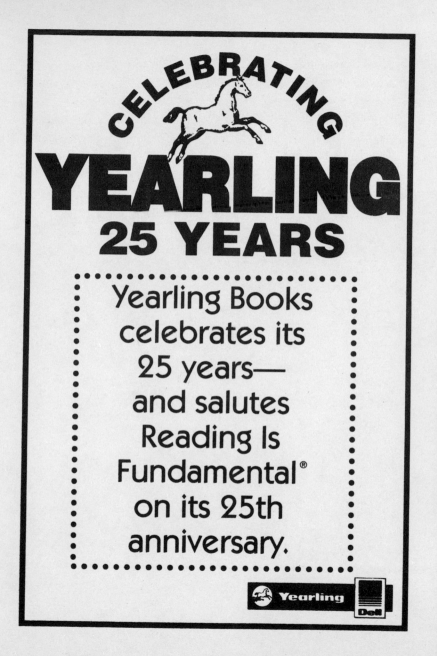